Rudyard Kipling

was born in Bombay in 1865 and educated
in England. When he was 17 he returned
to India, and there he began writing the
stories and poems that made him famous.
Kipling spent much of his life travelling,
and he was living in America when he wrote
The Jungle Book.

———————

Jonathan Mercer's woodcuts have been made
specially for Ladybird Classics. They are individually
hand-crafted from box-wood.

Ladybird books are widely available, but in case of
difficulty may be ordered by post or telephone from:

Ladybird Books – Cash Sales Department
Littlegate Road Paignton Devon TQ3 3BE
Telephone 0803 554761

A catalogue record for this book is available
from the British Library

Published by Ladybird Books Ltd Loughborough Leicestershire UK
Ladybird Books Inc Auburn Maine 04210 USA

Ladybird Classics

Tales from the Jungle Book

by Rudyard Kipling

Retold by Alison Ainsworth
Illustrated by Steve Lee
Woodcuts by Jonathan Mercer

A tiny brown baby came… out of the bushes

THE MAN-CUB

It was a warm evening in the jungle. In a cave high in the hills, Mother Wolf lay with her four cubs playing and tumbling around her. Father Wolf woke from his day's rest, yawned, and stretched his strong legs. It was time to go hunting.

Suddenly a blood-curdling roar filled the air. The wolves recognised that sound. It was made by a tiger, but not just *any* tiger.

Mother Wolf peered out of the cave. There was a rustling of leaves nearby. She stared in amazement as a tiny brown baby came crawling out of the bushes!

'Quickly, bring the little one to me,' she said to Father Wolf. At once, Father Wolf went to the baby. He picked him up as gently as he would pick up one of his own cubs. His sharp teeth didn't even mark the smooth skin.

He laid the baby at Mother Wolf's side. The baby sat up and smiled, and then he pushed between the cubs to get closer to Mother Wolf.

'How soft he is,' sighed Mother Wolf. 'And not in the least bit afraid of us.'

Suddenly the cave went dark. Shere Khan's great head and shoulders filled the entrance.

'What do you want?' asked Father Wolf, standing in front of Mother Wolf and the cubs.

'I was hunting a man-cub,' growled Shere Khan. 'His parents ran off. I saw him come this way. Give him to me!'

Father Wolf wasn't frightened. He knew that the huge tiger couldn't squeeze into the cave.

'The cub is ours now,' he said.

'How dare you! *Give me the man-cub!*' roared the angry Shere Khan.

At that, Mother Wolf sprang forward. 'The man-cub is *mine*!' she cried, her eyes blazing with anger. 'He shall not be killed by you. He shall live with us, as one of our own cubs. Leave us in peace. Go back to your own part of the jungle!'

Shere Khan knew that it was useless to argue. He backed out of the cave. But as he did so, he shouted, 'The man-cub *shall* be mine one day!' Then he stalked off down the hill.

'We won't let that tiger come near you again,' Mother Wolf said softly to the baby. The baby gurgled happily.

'What shall we call him?' asked Grey Brother, the eldest of the cubs.

'Let's call him Mowgli,' said Mother Wolf.

'And when he is grown up, he shall hunt Shere Khan,' added Father Wolf.

Mowgli laughed, innocently. He knew nothing yet of the adventures he would have as he grew up in the jungle!

At the top of the rock lay Akela, the leader of the pack

THE PACK COUNCIL

On the night of the full moon, Father and Mother Wolf took their four cubs and Mowgli to the Council Rock. This was a very special place. All new cubs had to be brought here to be inspected by the pack.

It was an anxious time for Mother Wolf. Mowgli had been a part of her family for two weeks now. She had grown to love him as much as her own cubs. But it was up to the pack to decide whether Mowgli could stay.

At the top of the rock lay Akela, the leader of the pack. Below him, in a circle, sat forty or fifty wolves, young and old.

In the centre of the circle, the new cubs were playing together. One by one the older wolves came forward. They had a good look at each cub.

At last they came to Mowgli who sat in the middle of the circle, playing with some pebbles.

Suddenly there came a roar from behind the rocks. It was Shere Khan.

'The man-cub is mine!' he growled. 'What do wolves want with a man-cub?'

Some of the younger wolves agreed. 'We don't want a man-cub in our pack!' they shouted.

'Silence!' commanded Akela. 'You all know the law of the jungle. If two members of the pack will speak for Mowgli, he may stay.'

Mother and Father Wolf looked all round the circle of wolves. If only someone would get up and speak for Mowgli! As they were his new mother and father, *they* were not allowed to speak for him.

The wolves sat quite still. Just as Mother Wolf thought that she was going to lose Mowgli, she heard a grunt behind her.

It was Baloo, the sleepy brown bear. His job was to teach the cubs the ways of the jungle. He was the only creature other than the wolves who was allowed to sit with the Pack Council.

He grunted again as he sat up. 'I speak for the man-cub,' he said. 'Let him run with the pack. I shall teach him.'

But Akela said, 'We need one more to speak for him.' Just then a dark shadow dropped down into the circle. It was Bagheera, the black panther.

'I come as a friend, Akela,' he purred. His voice was as soft and sweet as honey. 'I like the look of this man-cub,' he continued. 'If you let him stay in the pack, I will give you a whole bull. I have just killed him, and he is nice and fat.'

The wolves were always hungry. A whole bull would make a delicious feast. At once, they agreed to let Mowgli stay.

Shere Khan wasn't pleased. He gave a mighty roar, and vanished into the jungle.

Baloo taught him everything he needed to know

LESSONS WITH BALOO

Many years passed. Mowgli lived happily with the wolves. Mother and Father Wolf were very kind to him, and the four cubs thought of him as their brother. He grew bigger and stronger as he learned to live in the jungle.

Whenever he felt dirty or hot, he swam in the forest pools. When he was hungry he ate nuts and fruit, or honey from the wild bees. Soon he could climb almost as well as he could swim, and swim almost as well as he could run.

Every day Mowgli went to see Baloo. The wise old bear taught him everything he needed to know about the jungle.

Baloo taught him how to tell if a branch was rotten before climbing on it. He told him how to

13

speak politely to the wild bees if he came upon a hive. And Mowgli learned to warn the water snakes in the pools before diving in.

Then there were the hunting calls. Each creature in the jungle had a different call, and Mowgli had to learn all of them, in case he needed to call for help.

Often, if he hadn't learned what Baloo had taught him, the bear would smack him with his great paw. And sometimes Mowgli was naughty. Like most children he hated having to sit still all morning. Baloo became very cross when Mowgli fidgeted and wouldn't pay attention.

Sometimes Bagheera, the black panther, came to see how Mowgli was getting on. He would lie along a branch, purring gently, watching and listening.

One day Baloo smacked Mowgli just as Bagheera arrived. The little boy ran off in a temper.

Bagheera said, 'He is only little. He can't remember *everything* you teach him.'

But Baloo replied, '*No one* in the jungle is too little to be killed. He *has* to learn. That is why I sometimes give him a gentle smack.'

'Gentle!' snorted Bagheera. 'The poor child is covered with bruises from your "gentle" paws.'

'I was teaching him hunting calls this morning,' said Baloo, 'and he wasn't paying attention.'

'I should like to hear them,' said Bagheera. 'Where are you, Mowgli?' he called.

'I'm up here,' said a cross little voice above them. 'My head hurts.' Mowgli, still in a temper, came sliding down a tree trunk.

'Now, Mowgli,' said Baloo gently, 'let Bagheera hear the calls that I taught you this morning.'

At once Mowgli's face lit up. He loved an opportunity to show off.

'Calls for which creatures?' he asked. 'The jungle has many tongues. *I* know them all!'

'Very well, then,' laughed Bagheera. 'Tell me how you would call the kite.'

Without having to think about it, Mowgli put his hands around his mouth. A long, clear sound came from his lips.

'Very good!' said Bagheera. 'Now, how about the snake?'

Mowgli gave a low piercing hiss. Then he kicked his feet up behind and clapped his hands. He jumped onto Bagheera's back and sat drumming his heels against the glossy black fur.

How Bagheera and Baloo laughed at the little boy's antics! He had learned the calls *perfectly*. Baloo puffed up his chest with pride. Bagheera never showed his true feelings, but he was very proud too.

Mowgli bounced up and down on Bagheera's back. 'I shall have my own tribe! I shall be the leader!' he shouted.

'What *are* you shouting about, Mowgli?' asked

He jumped onto Bagheera's back

Bagheera. 'Stop jumping up and down and tell us.'

'Sometimes,' said Mowgli, 'when Baloo smacks me, the monkeys come down from the trees. They look after me. No one else cares about me.' He was close to tears.

'The *monkeys*!' snorted Baloo. 'They don't care about *anyone*.'

'They give me nuts to eat,' continued Mowgli. 'They say I shall be their leader one day. They have so much fun, Baloo. Why have you never taken me to meet them?'

Baloo looked down at him seriously. 'Listen very carefully to me, Mowgli,' he said. 'The monkeys are not to be trusted. They have no law, as we do. You must have nothing to do with them.'

Mowgli stared at Baloo. He had never heard him speak so gravely before.

'I'm sorry, Baloo,' he said quietly. Baloo gave him a hug. 'We'll say no more about it,' he said gently.

KIDNAPPED!

The morning's lesson over, Baloo and Bagheera settled down for their midday nap. Mowgli snuggled in between them. Soon all three were snoring gently.

Suddenly two large monkeys dropped down from the trees. They grabbed Mowgli's arms and legs and dragged him up into the treetops.

Still half asleep, the little boy struggled, but he couldn't get away. He tried to call for help, but his cries were drowned by the monkeys' howls.

As they carried Mowgli off through the jungle, branches and leaves flashed past, brushing against his bare skin. His face and body were soon covered in scratches.

The monkeys had hard little hands. They hurt

19

Mowgli's arms as they pulled him along.

As they leapt from tree to tree, Mowgli felt giddy. What if the monkeys were to let him fall? The ground was a *very* long way down.

Tears welled up in Mowgli's eyes as he thought of Baloo and Bagheera. Would he ever see them again?

Just then, the monkeys stopped to rest. Mowgli found himself at the top of a very tall tree. The jungle stretched out around him like a vast green ocean. And there in the blue sky above was Chil, the kite.

Mowgli took a deep breath. Then in a loud, clear voice he made the kite call that Baloo had taught him that very morning.

At once Chil flew down to see what was wrong.

'Please help me, Chil!' cried Mowgli. 'Find Baloo and Bagheera. Tell them where I am.'

Before Chil could reply, Mowgli was pulled back into the depths of the jungle.

Chil flew down to see what was wrong

THE COLD LAIRS

'Poor little Mowgli!' cried Baloo, hearing what had happened. 'What *are* we to do? We can't swing through the trees like monkeys!'

'I have an idea,' said Bagheera. 'We shall ask Kaa, the rock python, to help us to find Mowgli. He is the monkeys' greatest enemy. They are more frightened of him than of any other creature.'

They found Kaa stretched out on a warm rock. When he heard what had happened, he was only too happy to help. But where should they start looking for Mowgli?

Just then, a voice called out, 'Baloo! Baloo! Look up!' There above them was Chil the kite.

'I have seen the man-cub,' he cried. 'The

monkeys are taking him towards the Cold Lairs.'

Baloo looked at Bagheera in horror. The Cold Lairs! None of the jungle creatures dared go there – except the monkeys.

The Cold Lairs had once been a great city, built around a splendid palace. Now the place was no more than ruined houses and dark streets. Some said there were ghosts. The monkeys loved to play up and down the streets, pretending to be the kings and queens who had once lived there.

'It will take until this evening to reach the Cold Lairs,' said Kaa. 'We must go at once.'

Kaa and Bagheera set off first. Baloo followed as fast as his old legs could carry him.

Meanwhile, in the Cold Lairs, Mowgli was wandering among the ruined houses. He was very tired, but the monkeys would not let him sleep.

He was very hungry too, but the monkeys kept forgetting to bring food for him.

When Mowgli tried to escape, the monkeys put him in a marble summer house that was full of snakes. Luckily, Mowgli remembered the snake call. As soon as the snakes heard him, they knew he was a friend, and they didn't bite him.

Mowgli peeped through a hole in the wall. By the light of the moon he could just see the monkeys, sitting on terraces around the summer house. Each monkey took it in turn to stand in the middle and speak. A few monkeys listened but most were whooping and whistling, or throwing twigs and pebbles at one another.

Just then, the moon was hidden by a large cloud. In the darkness, a black shadow moved silently towards the terraces. Suddenly the shadow started hitting out with sharp, powerful claws. There was a terrific screeching and howling as monkeys were thrown in all directions.

Mowgli could hardly believe his eyes. What was happening over there?

There was a terrific screeching and howling

RESCUED!

A minute later, the cloud moved across the sky, and Mowgli saw that the shadow was Bagheera! Then he gasped as he saw twenty or thirty monkeys jump on top of the panther, biting, scratching and pulling him down.

Mowgli shouted at the top of his voice, 'Go to the water, Bagheera, the water!'

With all his strength, Bagheera struggled towards a small pond nearby. As soon as he splashed into the water, the monkeys jumped off his back. They hated getting wet. They danced up and down, waiting for Bagheera to come out.

Mowgli wondered what would happen next. Even Bagheera would not be able to fight off the monkeys alone. Where was Baloo?

Then Mowgli heard a low, rumbling roar. There was a clattering of stones, and Baloo heaved himself over the ruined city wall.

'I'm here at last, Bagheera!' he shouted. He flung his furry body at the crowd of monkeys by the pond. His paws flew around him, sending the monkeys flying through the air. Grabbing four or five at a time, he crushed them in a powerful bear hug.

But more and more monkeys came and threw themselves onto his huge back, pulling him down to the ground just as they had pulled Bagheera down.

Suddenly there came a sound that made everyone's hair stand on end. It was a long, low hiss that could come from only one creature.

The monkeys by the pond stopped dancing up and down. Those on Baloo's back jumped off. They all stared in terror as Kaa, the rock python, their deadliest enemy, came towards them.

Kaa was like a huge battering ram, throwing the screeching monkeys this way and that. Kaa's great tail curled round several monkeys at once and crushed the life out of them. The other monkeys ran for their lives.

As soon as he was free to move, Baloo broke down the door of the summer house. Mowgli threw his little arms round the bear's great neck. 'Poor Baloo!' he exclaimed. 'You're covered in bites and scratches.'

Bagheera climbed out of the water. His sleek black coat was scratched and bitten too. Mowgli was sad to think that his two friends had been hurt because of him.

Mowgli thanked Kaa for his help. 'I hope I can help *you* one day,' he said.

'You are a fine little man-cub,' Kaa said, smiling. 'Perhaps one day I *shall* need your help.'

Baloo and Bagheera started the long journey home. Mowgli, on Bagheera's back, slept soundly.

Mowgli thanked Kaa

THE RED FLOWER

Mowgli was now ten years old. His life in the jungle was never dull and very happy, for every day brought some new discovery.

Most of the time, Mowgli was with Bagheera. During the day they slept. Then, as night fell, it was time to go hunting. Mowgli loved to go into the deepest parts of the jungle. He was not in the least bit afraid when he was with Bagheera.

But Bagheera was worried. He had noticed that Shere Khan was spending more and more time with the young wolves in the pack. Akela, their leader, was getting old. Soon it would be time for a younger wolf to take his place. Without Akela to protect him, the wolves would drive Mowgli out of the pack.

Bagheera tried to explain this to Mowgli.

'But why should the wolves want to drive me away?' asked Mowgli. 'I have lived in the jungle all my life. I have obeyed the laws of the jungle. And it is to me the wolves come to have thorns pulled from their paws. Surely they are my brothers?'

Bagheera stretched out his neck. 'Little brother,' he said, 'feel under my chin.' Mowgli did so. Just under Bagheera's jaw he felt a bare spot where there was no black hair.

'I have that bare mark because for many years I had to wear a collar. The collar rubbed the hair away. No one here knows about my past. I was born in a cage, in the king's palace. My mother died there. I escaped and came to the jungle. But because I have lived among men and know their ways, I am feared by all the creatures of the jungle. Even Shere Khan fears me.'

'But I do not fear you,' said Mowgli.

'No,' replied Bagheera. 'You do not fear me. You are a man-cub. And just as I came back to the jungle to live, so you must return to the world of men. They are your *real* brothers. If you don't, you may be killed at the next Pack Council.'

'But why should the wolves want to kill me?' asked Mowgli, still puzzled.

'Look at me,' said Bagheera. Mowgli looked straight into Bagheera's eyes. The panther had to turn his head away.

'*That* is why,' he said. 'Not even *I* can look into your eyes, and I was born among men. The others hate you because of your eyes. They hate you because you can think for yourself. Most of all, they hate you because you are a man.'

Mowgli felt a lump rising in his throat. 'What must I do?' he asked, his voice trembling.

'You must go down to the village. Men grow a red flower there. Take some of it. Then the wolves will not come near you.'

Mowgli looked straight into Bagheera's eyes

Mowgli knew what the red flower was. It was the name jungle creatures gave to fire. He wasn't afraid of it.

He went down the hill to the village. There he saw a little girl holding a small pot full of red-hot coals. He ran up to her and snatched the pot away. Then he hurried back to the jungle.

He knew that he had to feed the red flower with dry leaves and twigs, or it would die. All day long Mowgli sat in the cave, feeding the red flower. At nightfall he made his way to the Council Rock.

Akela was not in his usual place. Instead, he lay by the side of the rock. That meant a new leader had to be found.

Shere Khan stood at the top of the rock. He started talking to the wolves as if *he* were the new leader. At once, Mowgli jumped up beside him. 'Why let a tiger lead you?' he cried. 'Wolves should be led by a *wolf*!'

At that, the younger wolves shouted, 'You are a man-cub! What right have *you* to stand on the Council Rock?'

'Let me take the man-cub,' Shere Khan growled, menacingly.

Akela lifted his head. 'Let the man-cub go in peace,' he said wearily.

Before the argument could turn into a battle, Mowgli picked up a branch and thrust it into the pot of red-hot coals. At once the flames leapt up. He held the blazing branch high above his head.

The wolves – and Shere Khan – gasped in terror and ran to hide behind rocks and bushes.

Mowgli stood alone at the top of the rock. 'I know that I must leave the pack,' he shouted. 'But I swear that I shall return one day. And when I do, I shall bring the skin of Shere Khan with me.'

As he said this, he leapt at Shere Khan and burned his whiskers with the flaming branch.

The tiger gave a yelp, then disappeared into the jungle. Most of the other wolves followed him.

Soon Mowgli was left with Bagheera, Mother and Father Wolf and his brother and sister cubs.

'Goodbye, little Mowgli,' said Mother and Father Wolf. 'We will never forget you.'

'And I shall always think of you,' said Mowgli, hugging Mother Wolf as if he would never let her go. His brothers and sisters were howling with sadness.

'I shall come and see you very soon,' promised Grey Brother.

Then Mowgli turned to Bagheera. 'I shall miss you terribly,' he whispered into Bagheera's ear.

Bagheera swallowed hard. 'Be brave, little brother,' he said. 'I shall always be here if you need me. Now go, quickly.'

Mowgli set off sadly down the hill. As he made his way to the village, he wondered what adventures his new life would bring.

'*I shall always think of you*'

VILLAGE LIFE

Mowgli arrived at the village just as the sun was rising. The man who came to open the gate to the village was most surprised to see a strange boy with long tangled hair sitting on the ground.

Mowgli was hungry, but he didn't know how to speak to the man. So he opened his mouth and pointed into it. The man stared at him, then ran back into the village.

He returned with the headman of the village, a fat man dressed in white. Soon everyone had come out of their houses to stare and point at Mowgli. One woman said Mowgli must be her long-lost son, who had been taken by a tiger when he was very small. Of course, Mowgli understood none of this.

The woman, whose name was Messua, took Mowgli home. She was kind to him, and gave him some milk and bread. They tasted very good.

Mowgli couldn't remember being in a house before. Messua pointed to a chair. 'Chair,' she said. At once Mowgli repeated the word. By evening he had learned many words.

That night Messua spread a blanket on a small bed in the corner. 'It's time to go to sleep,' she said. Mowgli got into bed and she tucked him in.

But Mowgli didn't like sleeping in a bed or having walls and a roof around him. In the cave he could look out and see the stars.

So he got out of bed quietly and climbed through the window. He lay down in the long cool grass next to the house. When Messua saw where Mowgli was sleeping, she wasn't angry.

In the middle of the night, Mowgli felt a soft nose on his cheek. It was Grey Brother!

'I bring news,' whispered Grey Brother.

'Shere Khan is very angry and has sworn that he will kill you.'

'I'm not frightened of him,' replied Mowgli. 'Will you come and see me often?'

'Yes,' said Grey Brother, 'I will wait for you in the bamboo that grows by the grazing ground.' Then he said goodbye and hurried back to the jungle.

For the next few months, Mowgli was very busy. There was so much he had to learn about man.

For one thing, he had to learn to use money. It seemed so important to the people of the village, but Mowgli simply couldn't understand the point of it. For another thing, he had to learn to plough and plant seeds.

Soon he could speak almost as well as the other children. But he sometimes mixed up words, and the children made fun of him. That made Mowgli angry, but life in the jungle had taught him never to lose his temper. Though he

There was so much he had to learn

was much stronger than the others, he never tried to hurt them.

One day the headman told Mowgli to take the cattle and buffaloes to the grazing ground. He was to help look after them all day, while they grazed.

Mowgli was pleased. Now that he had a job to do, he could sit with the men of the village. They held a meeting every evening, under a huge tree. It reminded Mowgli of the Pack Council.

One of the men, Buldeo, was the village huntsman. He sat with his gun across his knees and told tales of ghosts and goblins and strange happenings in the jungle.

The men's eyes nearly popped out of their heads as they listened to him. But Mowgli knew that such stories were not true. He also knew better than to say anything.

TIGER! TIGER!

The next morning Mowgli climbed onto the back of Rama, the great bull, and made his way to the grazing ground with his herd. There he saw the other village children who were looking after cattle.

The cattle moved around slowly, munching grass. The buffaloes wallowed in the muddy pools.

The children sat in the shade and played with pebbles, or wove baskets out of grass. They sang songs and made mud pies. When they felt tired they took turns to sleep.

As the sun began to set, the children called the herd together and went back to the village.

The days at the grazing ground were always

the same. How Mowgli missed the excitement of the jungle!

One day, when Mowgli was looking after the herd as usual, Grey Brother came running up to him. 'Shere Khan is coming for you!' he panted.

'Good,' said Mowgli. 'I shall be ready for him. We must split the herd in two, then trap him in the middle. But we need more help.'

'I have come to help you,' said a familiar voice.

'Akela!' cried Mowgli. He felt very proud to think that Akela had not forgotten him.

'Take one half of the herd, Akela,' said Mowgli. 'Grey Brother, you look after the other half.' The two wolves ran off at once to do as Mowgli asked.

Mowgli climbed onto Rama's back. Just then Shere Khan appeared. He started towards Mowgli, growling and baring his sharp teeth.

'Akela! Grey Brother!' shouted Mowgli.

There was a tremendous rumbling as the

Shere Khan... started towards Mowgli

wolves drove the herd forward. When Shere Khan saw the cattle and the buffaloes charging towards him, he knew he was trapped. He let out a long, loud roar.

But all his roaring couldn't help him now. With a thundering of hooves and a clashing of horns, the two halves of the herd came together. Shere Khan was trampled. A dense cloud of dust hung in the air.

When the village children saw what had happened, they ran home.

Mowgli started to skin the huge tiger. The wolves helped, with their sharp teeth.

The village children soon returned with Buldeo. The wolves hid before he could see them. Buldeo could hardly believe his eyes. A young boy skinning a ten-foot tiger!

'What's going on?' he demanded. 'Why did you let the herd stampede?'

Mowgli, busy with his knife, didn't answer.

'You have been a bad boy,' continued Buldeo. 'It was just lucky for you that the tiger happened to get in the way. There is a reward of one hundred rupees for his skin. Give me the skin, and I might give you one rupee to keep for yourself.'

'The skin is *mine*,' said Mowgli. 'I don't want your money. Go away.'

'How dare you speak to me like that!' exclaimed Buldeo. 'Let me have the skin!' At that, Grey Brother and Akela jumped out from behind the rocks. Buldeo was terrified.

'Let him go in peace, brothers,' cried Mowgli.

Buldeo turned and fled back to the village.

By the time Mowgli had finished skinning the tiger, it was almost dark. Akela and Grey Brother helped him to drive the herd back to the village.

All the villagers were waiting at the gate. Mowgli thought he would have a warm welcome.

After all, he had killed the mighty Shere Khan.

But the villagers looked angry. They threw stones at him. 'Go away!' they shouted. 'Take your evil magic back to the jungle, wolf-cub!'

Buldeo had told everyone that Mowgli must be a sorcerer. He said Mowgli had cast a spell over him, and that he had two enormous creatures at his side!

Mowgli couldn't understand what he had done that was so wicked. Why were the villagers angry with him? Then Messua came running up to him.

'My poor boy!' she cried. '*I* know you are good. But you must go back to the jungle. The villagers will kill you if you stay. Goodbye, dear son.' She kissed him, then she ran home, weeping.

Grey Brother pulled Mowgli off Rama's back. 'Come quickly,' he cried, 'before it's too late.'

So Mowgli and his wolf brothers ran all the way back to the jungle.

THE HOMECOMING

The sun was just rising when Mowgli came to Mother Wolf's cave. 'I have been driven out of the village,' he said, 'but I have kept my promise.' And he laid Shere Khan's skin at Mother Wolf's feet.

'I knew you would return one day,' she said, with tears of happiness in her eyes. 'And that you would kill Shere Khan.'

They all climbed up to the Council Rock. Mowgli spread out the huge tiger skin, and Akela lay down on it. Then he called the whole pack to the rock.

Mowgli stood at the top, next to Akela.

'I have come back!' shouted Mowgli. 'And I have kept my promise to kill Shere Khan!'

Mowgli and Grey Brother left the Council Rock

One old wolf called out, 'Lead us again, Akela! Lead us, man-cub!'

'Yes, yes!' called the other wolves. 'Let Akela *and* the man-cub be our leaders!'

'No,' replied Mowgli. 'I thought you were my brothers, but you drove me away. I thought the villagers were my brothers. They drove me away, too. I shall hunt alone from now on.'

'I will hunt with you,' said Grey Brother.

'And don't forget us, little brother,' said Baloo.

'Yes,' agreed Bagheera, 'we will always be there when you need us.'

So Mowgli and Grey Brother left the Council Rock together, and lived happily in the jungle they loved from that day on.